Backyard Barbecue
A Mike and Melanie Escapade, Book 4

Shannon Stiles

Table of Contents

Disclaimer

This book contains adult language and *very* explicit sexual content. It is not intended for nor suitable for anyone under the age of 18, nor for those who find this type of material offensive. If you fall into either of these two categories, please do NOT read this.

Backyard Barbecue
Foreword

Hey, Gang,

Melanie here. I just want to say hi and offer a *really* brief update for those of you who may be new to the series.

If you haven't been reading the escapades of Mike and Melanie since the beginning, well, shame on you – you should go back and start with book one. But if you don't have time, here's what you need to know as background in order to understand what's going on. All of these stories are about me, Melanie – Mel to her friends – and my boyfriend, Mike. We live together on West Eden Street, just up the hill from Kemperly Avenue, a main street through Springfield. He's 28, about 6'2" tall, and a self-employed stock trader who works from home. I think he's a hunk. I'm 23, 5'5" tall, 110 pounds with medium-long, blondish-brown hair. He thinks I'm hot. Oh, and we have an *open* relationship, meaning we're free to engage in hanky-panky with others. And we do!

My friend, Nikki, is single and lives across the street from us. She's a little bit taller than me and has blonde hair, which she usually wears in a ponytail. She runs an internet sex site from her house and makes a *lot* of money doing it. Guys like her – she's funny and sexy and cute – and she likes guys. She *really* likes guys.

And that's about all you really need to know. So, ... read on!

On the Sunday before the 4th of July, Mike and I threw a backyard barbecue and swim party for a few of our *adult* neighbors. No children allowed. We invited about 10 or 12 of the folks who lived around us, and most of them dropped by for at least a while, with the exception of the Jensen's, who lived right next door. According to Patti – Mrs. Jensen – she and George were prohibited from "partying" on Sundays because of their religious beliefs. Too bad. More barbecue for me!

Nikki from across the street, our slutty neighbor with the live internet sex show, came and brought her sometime assistant, Tim, whom Mike and I had never met. He turned out to look a lot different than the way Nikki had described him to us. She'd told us he was a nerdy little guy but Tim was anything but little. He was easily as tall as Mike – that would be either six-two or six-one, depending on whether you believed Mike or his driver's license. And he didn't look like a nerd, either. He was muscular and good-looking, with a beautiful smile and longish, wavy, light brown hair. That's something I always like on guys – long, but not too-long hair. Maybe this wasn't the same guy named Tim, I thought. Maybe Nikki called all her 'assistants' Tim, the way she called all her guests either John or Marcia.

Three other couples made the trip to our little shindig from next door or across the street – Fred and Claire, Elaine and Tom, and, perhaps the most interesting couple on the street, Arthur Ebblings and his hot trophy wife, Barbara. Or Bobbi, as she preferred to be called. She always introduces herself as, "Barbara, call me Bobbi." I'm sure there must be people out there who think her name is Barbara Calamibabbi and are wondering if that name is Italian.

Arthur was quite a bit older than the rest of us – mid-fifties, I'd guess, judging by his receding hairline and thinning hair. He was really short. I'm about five-five and he was shorter than me by an inch or so. He also had the beginnings of what's commonly called a *beer belly* – not really super-fat or anything gross, just getting started on it. And he showed up for our little *soiree* wearing one of those tiny, Speedo-style bathing suits, what the Australians call 'budgie smugglers.' That's a perfect name for them, in my opinion.

Bobbi was also a bit older than the rest of us, maybe 35 or 36. She was tall – way taller than her husband – slender and blonde, with big fake boobs about the same size as her head. She, too, was skimpily dressed, wearing a thong-bikini that showed her butt-cheeks and upper thighs to be nice and firm – obviously, she'd been exercising. When you saw her and Arthur together, 'trophy wife' is the thought that popped automatically into your head!

Anyway, Elaine and Tom and Claire and Fred didn't stay long – just a quick swim and a couple of hot dogs and they were on their way, off to attend to other, more-important business, I guess. By seven o'clock, only six of us – Nikki and Tim, Arthur and Bobbi, and me and Mike – remained, hanging around the pool and patio, drinking beer, smoking weed, and getting pretty fucked up. Well, it's not like anybody had to *drive* home!

"Anybody want anything more to eat?" Mike announced, as he made himself a last burger. "I'm gonna close this baby down."

Mike's offer found no takers – we were all comfortably full, apparently. Perhaps that's why conversation had come to a standstill. We were all too full, too drunk, and too stoned to engage in such a difficult activity as talking.

"I think I need a swim," Nikki's friend, Tim, announced. "Maybe sober up a little bit. Anyone want to join me?"

No one volunteered, so he got up and padded to the pool, alone, and dived in. I watched him as he splashed around in the pool. He really was a cute guy, not at all like Nikki had described him. And there he was, all alone in the pool ...

They say swimming alone is dangerous, you know, that you should always have a partner, in case you get into trouble. I don't know who 'they' are, but I'm sure they're right. And I certainly wouldn't want anyone to drown in our pool, especially Tim, now swimming laps about 30 feet away from me.

"I think I'm gonna take a swim, too," I said, staggering to my feet. I was *really* stoned. Alcohol is not really my drug of choice and, combined with all the dope I'd smoked and all the food I'd eaten, the three beers I'd put away had left me in a bit of a stupor. Hopefully, a splash or three in the water would clear my head.

I climbed down the ladder at the deep end just as Tim pulled himself up out of the pool and turned around to sit on the edge, dangling his feet in the water and watching me as I swam back and forth. Eventually, I swam over and stood there, in about three feet of water, right in front of him. "So, you're the famous Tim I've heard so much about," I said.

"Really? Famous, huh? That sounds interesting. What have you heard?"

"Well, that you're Nikki's assistant on her internet show, for one thing."

He chuckled. "Assistant?"

"Yeah, that's what she said. She said you were a college student and you set up her studio for her and you were an assistant on her show, sometimes."

"That's partially right. I am a grad student and that part about setting up the studio and being an assistant on the show sometimes is true. But I'm more than just an 'assistant.' Nikki and I are partners. I own 50 percent of the show and she owns 50 percent."

"Oh." That was a little surprising. "She also said you were a little, tiny guy. Are you the same Tim she was telling me about?"

He started laughing. "Yeah. I am. And she always describes me as a little tiny guy. It's an inside joke, just between the two of us."

"What? Tell me."

"Do you know what I do on the show?"

"Yeah. Help her demonstrate sex toys."

"That's right. And, ... uh, this is a little bit embarrassing, ..."

"Oh, go ahead. It's all right. I'm a big girl."

"Well, uh, ... I have a big dick."

"*Really?*"

"Yeah. And Nikki says my dick is so big it makes the rest of me look like a little tiny guy. That's the joke."

By this time I was less than a foot away from him, standing in between his legs with my forearms resting on his thighs. "Can I see?" I said.

"What?"

"Can I see your dick?" I glanced over his shoulder, where the other four members of our party appeared to be sleeping.

He turned to check on our comatose compatriots, then turned back to me and said, "Pull it out."

"You want *me* to pull it out?"

"Yeah. If you want to see it, reach in and pull it out." He grinned at me.

I guess he thought I wouldn't do it but ... he was wrong. My right hand slid up his thigh and under the leg of his bathing suit, then under the edge of that soft, built-in ball-supporter thingy. And there it encountered something of truly monstrous size. "Fuck!" I said as I wrapped my fingers around it. "That's big!"

"I told you. Big – that's how I got the *assistant* job."

I tugged that monster out the side of Tim's bathing suit, staring at it. No doubt about it – it was a *schlong*! And Nikki had been right when she'd called it 'attractive.' It was a handsome dick, smooth and straight and clean-looking, without a pubic hair in sight, which made it look even longer.

"It's nice," I told him, giving that gorgeous whoopie-stick a couple of appreciative squeezes, causing it to tense up.

"You want a taste?"

"Nope." I flicked the head with my finger and fell backward into the water, sculling away from him and laughing. Of course, what I'd told him was a complete lie – I *did* want a taste. His dick looked delicious and I would have loved to slurp it into my mouth and show him how well I could handle a schlong – my favorite word for a *really* big dick. Unfortunately, this was probably not the best time for that because, up on the patio, the rest of the gang seemed to be waking up.

The sounds of doors sliding open and of chairs scraping across concrete showed that someone was awake up there. I swam over to the side of the pool, next to Tim, to get a better look at what had brought our pooped-out party back to life, and was totally surprised by what I saw. Mike and Arthur each had a guitar and were apparently getting ready to play a duet. The guitars were Mike's – he had three of them but he seldom played and, to tell the truth, he wasn't very good. And Arthur? He certainly didn't look like a guitar player.

Bobbi and Nikki were offering encouragement – along the lines of, "Play something everyone knows so we can sing along," but the guys seemed to be having trouble finding a song they both knew how to play.

"C'mon," I said to Tim. "Let's go listen." I climbed out of the pool, grabbed a towel from a nearby chair, and dried myself off.

"Yeah, okay," he said, but he didn't move.

"You coming?"

"In a bit. I need to, uh, ... relax a bit more."

It was easy to see what he meant. The front of his swim trunks had a big bulge from where he'd tucked his schlong back into them. "Sorry about that," I said, laughing and thinking, *the cock-teaser strikes again!*

Arthur and Mike finally found a song they both knew how to play and, after a couple of false starts, staggered into a less-than-rousing rendition of *Puff the Magic Dragon*. I sat down next to Nikki, to listen, just in time to catch a hit from the joint she and Bobbi were smoking. After a couple of minutes, Tim, still kinda bulgy in the front, came over and sat next to me.

The guys were terrible, stumbling through the song, playing the wrong chords and faking the lyrics. It didn't matter. The four of us who knew we weren't guitar players sang along, laughing at mistakes, our spirits buoyed by our heavy intake of beer and weed.

The *Mike and Arthur Show* petered out after a couple of more songs, with both guys agreeing they were better at listening to music than playing it. It was starting to get dark, so everyone picked up and moved into the living room, gathering around the sofa and coffee table. Since both Tim and I were still wet from our swims, Mike got a pair of shorts for him to wear and I went into the bedroom and changed into a pair of white shorts and a white halter top, both designed to show off the gorgeous tan I'd acquired during the past month or so.

Once everyone was settled comfortably in the living room, we got into some serious smoking. We had four joints going at the same time, passing them around among the six of us, leaving little time for breathing pure air. I don't know about the others but, in no time at all, I was totally *ripped*!

As I sat there, I noticed that an interesting pattern had emerged. We had paired off into boy-girl couples but none of us were with our significant other. Arthur and Nikki were sitting together on the sofa and next to them were Bobbi and Mike, sitting *really* close together. Tim and I – the latecomers – were seated on the floor, on *zabutons*.

Conversation was minimal, and most of it was just comments about the quality of the weed and how relaxed everyone felt. Bobbi was the only one who seemed to have any energy, offering up observations on everything from the weather to politics, seemingly trying to pump some life back into our little get-together. Perhaps the most interesting thing that happened, though, started with a simple, everyday statement.

"I gotta go pee," Bobbi said.

I pointed down the hall. "Down there, on the left," I told her, and she trundled off in that direction.

Ten minutes later, Arthur noticed his wife was missing. "What happened to Bobbi?" he said.

"Bathroom," I said.

"That was like an hour ago."

"Lemme go knock on the door. See if she's all right," Mike, her sofa-partner, said. He hopped off the couch and trotted off, down the hall.

Ten minutes later, Arthur noticed that Mike was missing, and his wife *still* hadn't returned. "What happened to Mike?" he wanted to know. "And Bobbi."

"I'll go find them," I said, getting to my feet.

"Hurry back," Tim said.

"You betcha." I smiled down at him, then headed down the hall to find the missing couple.

The guest bathroom was empty, as was our bedroom and attached bathroom. There was no sign of either Mike or Bobbi. But as I headed back to the living room, intending to report that we had a genuine mystery on our hands, I heard a noise coming from a spare bedroom.

Our house had four bedrooms – the master bedroom plus three others. However, we only used one of the three as a guest bedroom. The other two served different purposes. One was Mike's 'office,' housing his computers and some stock-trading items, and the other was an exercise room that he had set up with a bench and some weights. It was from this latter room that the noise emanated. A dim light also peeked out from under the closed door.

I opened the door and said, "Mike?" I said. "Is that you?"

"Uh-huh," came the reply.

I went in. He was standing there, leaning against the wall, his shorts down around his ankles, smoking a joint. The missing Bobbi was on her knees in front of him, and his dick was in her mouth. "What's going on?" I said.

"Just having a smoke."

Bobbi never said a word. She gave me a quick sideways glance that seemed to say, "Leave us alone. We're busy," and kept slurping Mike's dick.

"It looks like you're getting a blowjob."

"Oh, that. Yeah. Bobbi wouldn't take no for an answer."

"I see. So, ... it's her fault?"

"Entirely."

"Anyway, you better wrap it up. Arthur's been wondering what happened to her."

"Uh, can you keep him busy for a while? So I can finish up here?"

"Lemme see if I've got this straight. You want me to distract Arthur so you can continue fucking his wife in the mouth – is that it?"

"Yeah. That's pretty much it." He passed the joint over to me. I took a hit and passed it back, watching Bobbi as she continued munching Mike's cock.

"How long?" I said.

"I dunno. Maybe, like, ten minutes."

"That seems like a long time."

"Well, she's doing such a good job and I'm really enjoying this, so, you know, it might take a while."

"Damn! Bobbi's just a regular little cocksucking slut, isn't she?"

Down below, at crotch level, Bobbi's head nodded up and down in agreement, causing Mike to flinch and say, "Uhnn!" as his dick slid out and then back into her mouth.

"So, go keep Arthur occupied or something, okay?"

"All right. But you owe me big-time for this." I started to leave, then turned back and said, "And wipe up the floor when you're done – where your new girlfriend is drooling all over it! And change your shorts before you come back, too." I pointed at a large puddle of spit that had collected on the floor and on Mike's shorts and then I left, pretending to be mad. Behind me, Bobbi continued doing what she'd been doing when I arrived – giving Mike that *extra-sloppy* blowjob!

When I got back to the living room, I went over to Nikki and whispered in her ear, "Keep Arthur busy for a few minutes. Okay?"

She gave me a quizzical look in return, so I stuck my thumb in my mouth, made a couple of sucking motions, and nodded toward the bedroom. The puzzled look was replaced by a smile and a nod. "You'll owe me," she said, glancing over at Arthur, who, truth be told, wasn't exactly a dreamboat.

"Yeah, yeah. Okay." This was getting complicated. Mike owed me – big-time – and now I owed Nikki, and I didn't even know what it was that was owed!

"Everything all right?" Tim said, when I sat back down, next to him.

"Uh-huh. I found them. They're, uh, ... busy."

"Busy?"

"Yeah. Mike turned one of our spare bedrooms into a weight room. They're in there. Bobbi's helping him with a ... muscle stiffness problem. Just helping him relax his stiff muscle, you know." I smiled at my cleverness in describing what was going on in that spare bedroom.

"Well, that's, ... interesting," he said, returning my smile.

We sat there, sharing a joint and watching Nikki as she attempted to keep Arthur from wondering what happened to his missing wife. She'd moved so close to him it looked as if she was trying to climb on top of him. Her mouth was up near his ear – from my angle I couldn't tell if she was talking to him or tonguing it – and her right hand was resting on that budgie-smuggler bathing suit. Arthur looked happy.

After a minute or two, I noticed there seemed to be a struggle of some kind taking place inside Arthur's swim suit, like something was trying to escape the confines of that tight, restrictive space. The front was bouncing around, threatening to rip the fabric. Nikki kindly lent a helping hand and tugged the front of his suit away from his tummy, letting the prisoner escape, so to speak.

The *prisoner* peeked over the top of Arthur's suit, took a look around, and apparently liked what it saw because it stretched out a couple of inches higher, no doubt to get a better view. Nikki took her index finger and lightly stroked the freed captive – just once, from bottom to top

– and it shot up another couple of inches, where it stood, semi-stiff, wobbling from side to side.

I knew Nikki had the cure for that wobbling problem and, sure enough, a couple of strokes of her hand brought the captive to full attention, revealing it to be, ... a *schlong*! Holy shit! All this time, tucked away in Arthur's tiny budgie smuggler was a monster dick! I immediately began to rethink my assessment of Bobbi as a trophy wife – maybe Arthur was Bobbi's trophy husband!

Nikki seemed both surprised and pleased at the results of her handiwork. She looked over at us and saw we were watching, so she wrapped her hand around the base of Arthur's dick and waved it at us. A fat four inches stuck up above her hand. It definitely qualified as a *schlong*!

"Let's go outside," I suggested to Tim.

"Outside? We'll miss the rest of the *Nikki Show*."

"That's okay. I need some fresh air to clear my head. I'm too stoned."

He scrambled to his feet. "Let's go, then," he said, helping me up.

As we headed out to the patio, I looked back at Nikki and Arthur, on the sofa. Nikki had apparently decided that schlongs were a good source of protein, as her head was bobbing up and down on Arthur's stiffy, looking for a snack. She saw me looking at her and gave me a little finger-wave goodbye. I waved back.

Tim and I curled up together on one of our comfortable chaise lounges. It wasn't really designed to hold two people, so we were pretty close together – so close that he had a hand on my left breast and I had a hand on his crotch. It was so crowded, there was just no place else to put them!

"Comfy?" I said.

"I am." He leaned over and kissed me, gently massaging my breast as he did so. When I responded, he added more passion to his kiss, as well as his tongue. Under my hand, I felt the schlong waking up.

"Oh, oh, I think trouble's brewing," I told him, giving his swelling member a couple of squeezes.

"Yeah, I guess he's recovered from your rejection, earlier, in the pool. He was a little depressed, you know."

"That was just a *temporary* rejection," I told him. "I didn't mean to hurt his feelings."

"He's kinda sensitive, actually."

Aren't they all? I thought. "Maybe I should apologize, then."

"Yeah, you probably should," he said. A huge grin was plastered across his face.

"Okay, bring him out here and let me apologize to him."

He reached into his shorts and the schlong came tumbling out, not yet fully erect, still in that in-between, spongy state, not quite sure of where we were heading and apparently not wanting to get *too* excited in case things didn't work out. I grasped it and pulled it upward, then leaned over and kissed the head, adding just a little, teeny-tiny bit of tongue. "I'm so sorry, Mr. Schlong," I said. "I didn't mean to make you feel sad." Then I tucked that rapidly-stiffening piece of meat back into his shorts.

"There. How's that?" I said. "Is he happy now?" I gave Tim an innocent smile and batted my eyelashes at him, but I don't think he noticed since we hadn't turned on the patio lights and the corner in which we'd chosen to kanoodle was pretty dark.

"Mr. *Schlong*? What?"

I laughed and explained the meaning of the word to him, eliciting a chuckle.

"So, ... what? That's it? That's your apology? You don't want a taste?"

"I do, but, ..."

"I know, you're shy. Right?"

I laughed. "Hardly. Maybe later. Right now I'm thinking I want to go for a swim."

"You're kidding, right?"

"Nope. C'mon, it'll be fun. And maybe it'll clear the fuzz out of my head."

"My trunks are in the house. And these are Mike's shorts."

"Take 'em off. We'll go skinny-dipping."

"Okay, but you first."

"What? You don't trust me?" I said, pretending he'd hurt my feelings.

He laughed. "I just met you. I don't even know you."

"That's what makes all this so exciting." I removed my top and shorts, laid them on a chair, and stood there for a few seconds, naked, making sure he got as good a look as the dim light from a cloudy moon would allow. Then I crossed over to the pool and slipped into the warm, heated water.

Tim followed, sliding into the water behind me. I swam over to the side of the pool and waited for him to catch up.

His dick – no longer spongy but hard and sticking out, like the limb of a tree – pressed up against my butt as he wrapped his arms around me and kissed the back of my neck, making me shiver. I turned around to face him. "You know, I think you were right, earlier," I said.

"Right about what?"

"My apology to your schlong. It really wasn't very good, as far as apologies go."

"Would you like a do-over? I'm sure he'd be willing to give you a second chance."

"You know, I think I would. Why don't you sit up here on the edge, like you were this afternoon, and let me try again?"

"All right." He pushed himself up, out of the water, twisting around at the same time so that he ended up seated on the edge of the pool with his legs spread apart. The monster known as Schlong stared up at me, waiting for my apology, as I stood before it.

"I'm really sorry, Mr. Schlong," I began, wrapping my fingers around that huge piece of meat and using it to pull myself closer, until I was standing between Tim's legs. "I didn't mean to make you sad. And I hope we can be friends." I leaned over and sucked just the head of that whoopie stick into my mouth, running my tongue over it.

Tim responded with a long, "Ummmmmmm," and leaned back, bracing himself with his arms. "I knew you were my kind of girl," he said.

"You sure Nikki didn't mention anything to you about me?" I said, but since I had a rather large dick in my mouth, it came out sounding like, "Oo foo thikky thidn minthn idithn foo oo fabow meu?"

"What?" he said.

I spit his dick out into my hand, massaging that monster as I repeated myself.

"She might have mentioned you. I think she said you were cute. Oh, and friendly."

Yeah, I'll bet she put the word 'dick' in front of 'friendly,' too, I thought. I was beginning to think Tim accompanying Nikki to our little pool party today was a setup – that she'd brought him along just to distract me. I knew she had a bit of a crush on Mike, and if I was busy with Tim, she'd have a chance to hook up with him. Since I found Tim to be kinda hot, it was a pretty good plan, I guess, except for one thing – Bobbi had already claimed Mike for herself, leaving Nikki stuck with Arthur.

I gobbled the schlong back into my mouth and went to work, sipping and sucking and slurping, giving that monster the apology it felt it deserved. Tim watched me, offering occasional comments on my skills and on the effects they were having on him. "Oh, that's good," he said. "Do that again, I like that." And, my favorite, "You're really very, very good at this."

How about that? Two verys – not just very good, but very, very good! "Thanks," I said. "I take pride in my work," but that also came out as unintelligible gibberish, for the same reason as before. I'm really going to have to learn not to talk with my mouth full.

After a while, Tim's dick became slightly agitated, a warning of what was likely to happen if I kept doing what I was doing, so I released it and slid down the shaft for some ball sucking. I slurped first one, then the other, into my mouth and sort of squished them around in there, as if they were grapes or cherry tomatoes. At the same time, my hand slowly milked the schlong, hopefully just enough to keep him interested but not so interested that he'd cum!

And then Tim said, "I've got an idea. Why don't we trade places?"

"Oh-kay." *I thought you'd never ask!*

He hopped down into the water, next to me, and hoisted me up by my waist, setting me down in the spot he'd just vacated. I like to think of myself as a helpful person so, in an effort to be user-friendly, I spread my legs open just about as far as they'd go. Tim seemed to appreciate the gesture.

"That's beautiful," he said, standing there in the water and staring at my pussy.

"Is that your thing?" I said.

"What?"

"Gawking at pussies. Do you get off just looking at them?"

He laughed. "Yeah, that's kind of a turn-on. But I do more than just look, a *lot* more."

"I'm glad to hear that," I told him.

He grabbed me by the hips and pulled me toward him, across the smooth tiles lining the rim of the pool, until my butt was right on the edge. Then he spread my pussy lips with his fingers and, starting at the very bottom, ran his tongue slowly up my wet, eager slit until it bumped into my clit, where it performed a sort-of inspection that included a lot of poking. It then retreated along the same path, back down my slit to the bottom, only to repeat the same maneuver, over and over and over again.

Initially, I thought perhaps Tim's pussy-eating abilities were, how shall I put this nicely – somewhat *limited*? It was just the same thing, repeated again and again, without variation – tongue slides up my slit, pokes my clit and retreats, then does it again. But somewhere around the 25th or 30th trip up my slit – which was now producing juice at an alarming rate, by the way – I changed my mind. I realized Tim's technique wasn't limited, it was *fabulous*, especially that part where his tongue kept bumping into my clit and then exploring it, as if it didn't know what it was that was blocking its path. That one little move alone was driving me crazy. I could feel the electricity building in my body as a storm started to build in my fingers and toes.

I grabbed a towel laying on the pool deck next to me, positioned it behind me and leaned back, putting my feet up on his shoulders. Hey, there's no rule that says a girl can't be comfortable while she's getting her slit slopped. Right? I also closed my eyes, the better to concentrate on Tim's munching maneuvers.

So I was lying there, really, *really* enjoying the travels of Tim's tongue, when a voice from above me said, "And just what's going on here, young lady?" I opened my eyes and looked up to see Nikki, smiling down at me.

"Oh, Tim and I are just, uh, checking each other out. Getting to know one another."

"I see. And how's that going?"

"Pretty fucking good, actually." Down between my legs, Tim mumbled something that sounded as if he agreed with me. It tickled.

From behind Nikki, another female voice said, "Well, well, and what do we have here?"

I leaned my head back just in time to see Bobbi, with Mike in tow, arrive on the scene. Damn! My quiet, private introduction to Tim and his schlong had turned into a live sex show and there wasn't any good way to lie my way out of this – we'd been caught! So I said, "Good evening, everyone. And welcome to tonight's show. I see we're all here – oh, wait. Where's Arthur, Nikki?"

"He's asleep on the sofa. You said to keep him busy, so I hypnotized him."

"Ooh, hypnosis. Does that involve using your mouth?"

"Sometimes. There are lots of ways to do it."

Tim finally came up for some fresh air and to greet our *guests*. "Hi, gang," he said.

"So, don't let us interrupt you," Nikki said.

"Yeah," Mike chimed in. "Just pretend we're not here and go back to what you were doing."

I sat up. "This isn't working," I told Tim. "I'm not used to performing for an audience. I think we need to go back inside."

"Yeah," Bobbi said. "Let's all go inside and have an orgy."

"Now there's a good idea," Nikki said. "A great big, suck and fuck orgy."

"That's not exactly what I had in mind," I told them.

Nikki helped me to my feet and, shy girl that I am, I picked up the towel I'd been lying on and wrapped it around me. "Oh, c'mon," she said. "Don't be a party pooper. Orgies are fun."

"I know, but ..." I glanced down at Tim, still in the pool. I suspected he was waiting for the schlong to relax a bit before joining us landlubbers. "Whaddaya think?" I said.

"Up to you. I'm good with whatever you want to do."

"All right," I announced. "We'll have an orgy, but only on one condition – everyone strips naked, right now."

No one moved.

"I mean it," I said. "Tim and I aren't going to be the only ones marching into the house in our birthday suits. I want to see tits and dicks – now!"

Bobbi stepped forward. "I'm game," she said, and that skimpy bikini she still had on came off in less than 10 seconds. She put her hands behind her head and shook her gigantic fake books at us, getting a laugh. It's funny the way they're able to stick straight out like that, with no sag at all, defying gravity.

"Well, never let it be said I'm the one holding up the orgy," Nikki said, stripping off her clothes and dropping them on the deck. When she was naked, she turned around and tugged Mike's shorts down, leaving him wearing just a shirt and a grin.

"Take off your shirt," I said. "You look ridiculous."

He removed his shirt and tossed it into the pile of clothing on the deck. "Happy now?" he said, and stuck his tongue out at me.

Tim climbed out of the pool and unwrapped the towel from around me, using it to dry himself. The schlong had returned to a more-relaxed state, just a big hunk of meat, hanging between his legs, waiting to be fluffed up again. Hopefully, I'd be the one to play fluffer.

"So?" Nikki said. "Everyone's naked. Let's go." She headed toward the house and the rest of us fell in behind her, snaking our way across the patio. If we'd added music and grabbed the hips of the person in front of us, we could have passed for a conga line – a *naked* conga line.

Nikki slid open the glass door leading into the living room but before going inside, she stopped, turned around and said, "What about Arthur? Should we wake him up or what?"

"No, let him sleep," said Bobbi. "He's old – he needs his beauty rest."

"Okay, then. To the bedroom." Our procession continued, advancing into the living room.

Arthur was sprawled on the sofa, naked, his legs apart – not an especially attractive picture, I might add. His tiny, budgie-smuggler swimsuit was on the floor in front of him and he was snoring away, peacefully, with a smile on his face. His dick was limp and about half the size it was when Nikki waved it at us, earlier. Judging by the evidence in front of us, that dick appeared to have been recently drained.

"Hypnosis, huh?" I said, quietly, to Nikki as we passed.

"I told you, there's lots of ways to do it," she whispered back.

When we got to the bedroom, Mike, Bobbi, and Nikki all clambered up onto the bed, but I steered Tim onto the soft, comfortable, two-seat couch that faces our bed from about eight feet away. Mike and I sometimes jokingly refer to it as our *viewing couch*, based on how it had been used during previous parties held in our bedroom. It offered both a tiny modicum of privacy and an excellent, unobstructed view of action on the bed!

I snuggled up next to him, taking the schlong in my hand – just holding it and giving it an occasional squeeze. Up on the bed, the rest of our would-be orgy participants had gone right to work, apparently not even noticing that Tim and I hadn't joined them. Mike was on his back and Nikki was lying next to him, and they were ... *kissing!* How romantic. Well, I'd known for some time that Nikki had a bit of a *thing* for Mike, but I wasn't worried – let her have her fun!

Not to be left out, Bobbi had commandeered a position between Mike's legs that offered excellent control of his cock. And controlling it she was – holding it around the base so that it stuck straight up in the air, where she was licking it, running her tongue up the shaft but stopping just short of the head. Technically, that technique comes under the heading of *cock-teasing*, I believe.

Thanks to the teasy-squeezy ministrations of my right hand, Tim's schlong had firmed up nicely. It was still a little on the spongy side, but I knew just how to fix that. I leaned over and slurped it into my mouth, sucking on the head.

Tim moaned and slumped back against the couch, sliding his hips forward. Not wanting to release the schlong from where it was being held captive by my mouth, I went along for the ride, ending up in a somewhat problematic, U-shaped position, with my head down below Tim's stretched-out-straight legs while I was still sitting on the couch. I solved that slight complication by swinging one leg up and over Tim's head, pulling his legs up onto the couch and turning him sideways. Then I planted my pussy firmly onto his mouth, giving us a near-perfect 69 configuration.

And then I sucked. I mean, I put some *serious* effort into getting the schlong back into tip-top, hard-as-a-rock shape. It didn't take long. I alternated between long, slow slides up and down the shaft and tonguing the head, and in just a few seconds, that spongy monster was transformed into a first-class stiffy, dancing in my mouth each time my tongue caressed its head.

Tim moaned into my pussy and mumbled something that sounded like," Ohhhhh, you're going to make me cum!"

Yup, that's the whole strategy behind sucking cocks – make 'em cum! I spit into my hand for lubrication and milked the schlong as I nibbled the head, tonguing it and scraping my teeth lightly across the tip. Meanwhile, down between my legs, Tim's tongue temporarily had forgotten its duties as pussy-licker and was now engaged in full-time moaning and making complimentary comments about my cocksucking technique. "Oh, that's good!" and "I like that!" and – my new favorite – "Five fucking stars!" he said.

Since not much was happening down in pussy-land, I climbed off him and down onto the floor, pulling his legs with me so that he ended up in a slouched, seated position and I ended up kneeling between his legs. This has always been my favorite blowjob position – I like to watch the reactions on the guys' faces as I suck their cocks and they like to watch me suck them, so it's kind of a win-win situation.

Once I had maneuvered the two of us into position – and not once did the schlong escape the confines of my mouth while I was doing it, I'm proud to say – I got back to work, milking and sucking and trying to smile once in a while, just to let him know I was enjoying this, too. Smiling with a schlong in your mouth, by the way, is *not* that easy, so mostly it was just milking and sucking.

Whatever. Even without a lot of smiles, Tim seemed to be having a pretty good time. The schlong was dancing around in my mouth, obviously getting ready to do what schlongs do – cum. Typically, when a big dick cums, it gifts you with a *large* donation of gooey goodness. So, as the schlong – which definitely qualified as big – began to throb and spasm, my mouth got ready to receive a big burst of dick-juice.

In my experience, guys cum in one of three different ways. I thought of them as *the blast, the spurt,* and *the gentle delivery.* The blast came from a dick that just explodes in your mouth, delivering 98% of its load all at once, with the rest just kind of dribbling out as an afterthought. My boyfriend, Mike, was the second kind, a spurter, pumping out his cock custard in a series of short, spasmodic squirts, sometimes numbering as many as a dozen. And with dicks that offered a gentle delivery, cum just sort of oozed out the end in a long, slow delivery. Basically, I was fine with all three methods, as long as I was *prepared* for what was coming.

So, as the schlong got ready to deliver the goods, I was ready and expecting a large load to be delivered. I just didn't know what the method of delivery would be. But if I'd had to guess, I would have picked *the blast*. However, that's not exactly what happened.

I was tongue-flicking the schlong's head when Tim announced, "I'm gonna cum!" Immediately I switched to full-on sucking and milking mode, pumping that pecker mercilessly, ferociously feasting like the famished fellatrice I was pretending to be. The schlong never stood a chance against my oral assault.

Tim leaned back, arched his body a bit, said, "Uhnnnnnnnnnn," and – surprise, surprise – laid a long, long, *long* gentle delivery onto my tongue. It seemed as if cum was coming out the end of that monster for a couple of minutes, although in actuality it was probably only about 10 or 12 seconds. Still, that was a lot of cum. A *lot*! And it tasted good, too. In fact, it might have been the best-tasting cum I'd ever had in my mouth. It had a tangy-sweet taste, not peppery or salty, like most cum.

I swallowed and kept swallowing until the schlong surrendered and began to retreat, shrinking as it did so. Then I licked it clean of Tim's tasty treat and kept right on licking and sucking as it slowly melted away in my mouth.

"Fuck! That was great!" Tim said. "You do that *real* good!"

I released the schlong and said, "Thanks. But I think I killed him. Look!" I showed him his dick, which had shrunk to a shadow of its former self.

"You can't kill Timmy," he said. "He's just resting up for future opportunities."

"Oh. Okay. And his name is Timmy?"

"Uh-huh. Little Tim, Little Timmy, Timmy – he answers to all of them. He's my friend and constant companion."

"Interesting." I climbed back up onto the couch, lay my head down on Tim's tummy and sucked Little Timmy back into my mouth, lightly nibbling the head as I watched Mike getting a double blowjob from Nikki and Bobbi, up on the bed. Tim's dick had more nicknames than any dick I'd ever encountered – five if you counted the two I'd given it, *monster* and *schlong*. And it also produced an excellent, sweet-tasting product when you milked it.

As I lay there, trying to munch the schlong back to life, I began to wonder what Tim thought about the way my pussy tasted. I once had a guy tell me that pussies came in only two flavors – banana and fish. And then he told me that mine had the ripest banana taste *ever*. I guess that was a compliment – I took it as one. It was certainly better than being told my pussy had the ripest fish taste ever!

I turned my head to look at him, leaving my hand in charge of trying to bring Little Timmy back to life. "Your cum tastes yummy," I told him. "Nice and sweet."

"So I've been told," he said. "Thanks."

"How come? Is there a secret?"

"I dunno. I always thought it was because I eat a lot of sugar."

"Sugar, huh?"

"Yup."

"Maybe I should try that. Go on a high-sugar diet. Get myself a really sweet-tasting pussy."

"No need for that. Your pussy tastes terrific, just the way it is."

"Yeah? What does it taste like?"

"Oh, I don't know. It tastes like, you know, ... delicious pussy," he said, grinning at me.

"C'mon, don't fool around. Tell me. I want to know what it tastes like – what *you* think it tastes like."

He thought about it for a while, then said, "Banana pudding. It tastes like nice, creamy, delicious banana pudding!"

Banana pudding. An excellent choice, Tim. Excellent! I smiled, extremely glad he didn't say, "Fish," turned around and resumed my pecker-plumping activities.

Meanwhile, up on the bed, Mike's double blowjob had morphed into a, … well, what would you call that, anyway? A bicycle built for two? A double cowgirl? Whatever it was, Mike was on the bottom, playing the part of the bike or the horse, and Bobbi and Nikki were the riders. Bobbi was perched on Mike's face, holding onto the bed's headboard as she rocked back and forth, grinding her pussy against his mouth. Nikki sat firmly astride his cock, bouncing up and down with considerable enthusiasm. It appeared the two of them were doing just fine and didn't need any help, so I stayed where I was, curled up on the couch with Tim's stiffening dick in my mouth, and watched the show.

"You're not jealous?" Tim said, pointing at the action on the bed.

"Nope," I said, dropping his dick into my hand for the sake of clear speech. "I have full access to that dick any time I want it."

"That's not what I meant. Doesn't it bother you, watching him up there with Nikki and Bobbi?"

"Not really. He's having a good time – enjoying himself. I'm happy for him. And I'm having fun, too, so he's happy for me, I assume. That's the way we feel about it."

"Amazing," Tim said. "So, then, he wouldn't be upset if I spread your legs and plonked my dick into that bowl of sweet banana pudding you keep down there?"

"Well, he wasn't upset when he saw me slurping away on your schlong, so I doubt a little pussy pumping would bother him, either. And it certainly wouldn't upset *me!*"

He smiled. "I need a little bit more work on Tim Junior, then."

Tim Junior, huh? Wow! That has to be a record – six nicknames!

"Not a problem," I said, and resumed my cock-chomping activities, sipping and sucking as *Tim Junior* steadily grew in both size and stiffness. While I munched, Tim lightly rubbed my upper back and the back of my neck, an extremely sensitive area of my body. To tell the truth, that felt almost as good as when he was slurping my pussy. My toes began to twitch and tingle.

After a few minutes of frolicking with my tongue and my lips, the schlong was back, just as stiff and ready for action as it had been before I'd drained it. Tim said, "You got a favorite position?"

I sat up. "You mean, other than having your dick in my pussy?"

He chuckled. "You know what I mean."

"I've always been fond of missionary," I said. In my opinion, you just can't beat good old, face-to-face fucking. But riding, cowgirl style, comes in a close second.

"Let's give that a try, then." He got down on the floor and pulled me forward on the couch, spreading my legs apart.

As I lay there, sort of scrunched up on the couch, a slight spasm shook my entire body. A sign of things to come, I hoped, anticipating my pussy's introduction to the schlong. I wriggled myself into a more-comfortable position, ready to welcome Tim's big banana to my banana basket.

Tim, however, had other ideas. He leaned forward, placed his mouth directly above my pussy, and spread it apart with his fingers. Then he left his mouth there, not doing anything with his tongue, just gently breathing warm air down across that juicy slit. Fuck! That felt wonderful, too. I moaned as the tingly feeling in my toes spread to my finger tips.

His tongue joined the action, sliding up my slit while he made slurpy noises, as if he was eating delicious banana pudding and just couldn't get enough of it. Nikki calls that *slit slurping,* which I think is a perfect description. "Just making sure things are nice and juicy," he announced. "We wouldn't want to hit any dry spots."

Dry spots? Are you kidding? There <u>are</u> no dry spots, anywhere down there. You could explore my sweet vag from one end to the other and I guarantee you wouldn't find a dry spot anywhere! That's what I meant to say. However, it came out as, "Ohhhhh! Uhhnnnnn! Fuck!!"

After a minute or so of Tim's tongue lapping my slit, I was ready to go. Fuck, I was ready to go before he even started! If I could have reached the schlong, I would have grabbed it and stuffed it in my pussy. "Fuck me, Tim," I said. "Fuck me good!"

He straightened up and moved closer to me, lining up his dick on my slit, now so juicy it could have doubled as a banana pudding factory. But instead of immediately sticking it in, he began with a little slit sliding, letting the schlong skate back and forth between my pussy lips. In response, my legs and arms started to lose feeling and a volcano commenced rumbling deep inside my body.

And then he slipped it in, the schlong sliding slowly into position. It wasn't a shock or anything like that – I've had giant cocks up my pussy before and I've gotten used to the way they feel as they ... kinda spread you open. To tell the truth, I *love* the full feeling you get from a really, really big dick.

Tim went to work, rocking back and forth at an unhurried, measured pace, not forcing anything, just letting the schlong and my pussy get to know each other. That was appreciated. It's more than a little uncomfortable when a guy is in a hurry and just jams his dick into you and starts banging away. The way Tim was doing it – just proceeding leisurely to get things going – was perfect.

Of course, a leisurely pace is just a starting point. And as the schlong gradually increased its pumping speed, the rumblings of the volcano inside me increased and lava began to bubble over the edges. I was heading for an eruption!

I grabbed Tim by the hips and joined him in his thrusting motions, pushing myself forward to meet each plunge forward of the schlong. The lava from the volcano was flowing now, wandering throughout my body and making it feel as if parts of me were on fire. I moaned and offered valuable, informative commentary on the way I felt. "Ohhhh. Ohhhhhhhh. Ohhhhhhhhhh!" I said, followed by a string of words beginning with the letter F.

Tim watched me, a smile on his face, as he buried the schlong deep inside me with each plunge forward. "Feel good?" he said.

"Fuck, yes! Good good! I'm gonna cum!"

And then he did something I wasn't expecting. He leaned forward, slid his hand under me and stuck his finger up my butt, just as I started to cum. That was all it took – the volcano erupted! "Oh! Oh! Oh!" seemed to be the extent of my vocabulary as hot lava spewed out and flooded my body, causing every part of it to tingle and shiver. Volcanic eruptions aren't supposed to cause that, are they? Tingles and shivers, I mean.

I tend to bounce around and, well, just *flail* a bit when I cum. And that's what I was doing. My arms flopped wildly about, as if they were trying to escape the hot lava that was about to consume them. My pussy shifted into what I like to call *meat-grinder mode* as it attempted to pulverize the schlong.

Tim stopped to watch. I gained just enough control of my arms and hands to grab him by the ass and pull him tight into me, holding him there as all the tension that had been building up inside the volcano was released. As the lava slowly flowed away and my body began to cool, every bit of stress and worry went with it, replaced by a feeling of deep, deep relaxation. And then Tim resumed stroking.

"Stop!" I said, my speech suddenly coherent again. "Don't move!"

"What's wrong?"

"Nothing. Just don't move!"

"Am I hurting you?"

"Shh, don't move. I like it when you don't move."

A puzzled look slid across his handsome face but he did as I asked, keeping perfectly still. I think he might even have been holding his breath. After 30 or 40 seconds, I said, "That's good," and I relaxed.

He immediately went back to the pussy-pumping game he'd been playing before we were so rudely interrupted by that volcano thing. However, he only managed to pump three or four strokes before I had another orgasm. This one was not the earth-shaking volcanic eruption that had flooded my body just seconds earlier, just a few spasms and shakes and renewed relaxation.

This time Tim knew just what to do, though. He kept the schlong in place and held it completely still until I visibly relaxed. *Good boy, Tim,* I thought. *And a quick learner, too!*

But good-boy Tim and his constant companion, Little Timmy, had more in store for me. Once I relaxed, he slipped both hands under my butt and stood up, taking me – still impaled on the schlong – with him. I wrapped my legs around him for support as the schlong sank deep into my pussy.

I don't know if this position has a name – maybe *standing cowgirl*, or something like that – but I do know it offers deep penetration, and I like that. After letting me wriggle around a bit to get comfortable, Tim lifted me up a few inches and then let gravity bring me sliding back down the schlong. And then he did it again. And again. I felt like commenting on the way I felt, but the only thing I could think of to say was, "Ohhhhh!" So I said it. More than once, as a matter of fact!

We settled into a rhythm. He'd lift me up and during the slide back down, I'd comment. So it went like this – lift up, slide down, "Ohhhhh!" lift up, slide down, "Ohhhhh!" lift up, slide down, "Ohhhhh!" – again and again.

Over Tim's shoulder, I could see the group on the bed. All three of them were watching me as I bounced up and down on the schlong, moaning, groaning, and throwing out an occasional scream, in addition to that one word, 'ohhhhh,' which I seemed to be trying to memorize. Nikki was wearing a big smile and was silently clapping, apparently cheering me on.

"Fuck you assholes!" I yelled at them. "Mind your own business!" Of course, I was smiling as I said it and my comments got laughs from all of them. I wrapped my arms around Tim, closed my eyes and buried my face in his shoulder, ignoring the voyeurs on the bed. Then I concentrated on what was important to me at this time – desperately trying to find another volcano before Tim got too tired to hold me up in the air.

No second volcano showed up, but I found something just as good – maybe better. I'm not even sure how to describe it. It was like one of those scenes you see on the news, where they're about to demolish a building by blowing it up and they're counting down, 10, 9, 8, like that, until they can push the plunger or whatever and the building goes BOOM! I was the building, awaiting that impending explosion, and with each slide down the schlong, another number of the countdown disappeared.

Even though I could feel it coming, I wasn't fully prepared for what happened. As the count diminished, I sped up, ignoring the lift from Tim's hands and doing all the work myself. Up, down, up, down, I went, pumping that pecker faster and faster as Tim struggled to stay on his feet.

And then, the count reached zero, someone pushed the plunger and things went BOOM! And BANG! And THWACK! as the building – me – exploded. My legs unlocked from where I had them wrapped around Tim' waist and shot straight out and began to shake uncontrollably. I let go of Tim's shoulders and arched backward, leaning over so far I would have fallen were it not for the support of the schlong and the fact that Tim caught me just as I started to head for the floor. The shaking in my legs spread to the rest of my body.

Tim's legs were a wee bit wobbly as he set me back down onto the edge of the couch, as gently as he could, and knelt in front of me. I could see him looking at me with concern as my entire body continued to just *vibrate!* I wanted to tell him I felt fine, great, wonderful, but I was unable to access the language part of my brain at the time, so I tried to smile.

He apparently took that as a signal to continue and the schlong, which had never lost its place during our position reshuffling, resumed its rhythmic ramming of my poor, defenseless pussy, this time with a sense of urgency. And then, before I even had a chance to fully recover from my full-body shakes, another explosion took place. Apparently the building was not completely destroyed by the first one. Or maybe I was having a *deja vu* experience. For whatever reason, another, slightly smaller but no less enjoyable blast took place.

This time, however, Tim did not stop pumping to let me enjoy what felt like my 17th or maybe 30th orgasm. I probably wouldn't have tried to stop him, anyway, but it's not like I had a choice. He had hold of my hips with both hands and was putting serious effort into his cock-plunging maneuvers, sliding the schlong in and out of my pussy with a determined look on his face. I knew what was coming and, since I really wasn't in a position to change the immediate future, I decided to make the most of the inevitable.

"Fuck me, Little Timmy," I whispered in Tim's ear. "Fuck me good. Fill me up with cum!"

"That's ... what ... I ... intend ... to do!" he said, plunging the schlong deep and holding it there as it throbbed and released its payload. I managed to squeeze out one last, tiny explosion at the same time.

This really hadn't been part of the plan. To let him cum in my pussy, I mean. But it happened and I must admit, afterward, the sensation of the schlong shrinking and slowly retreating from inside me felt terrific. And once again, of course, pussy beats dick – it *always* happens that way!

Tim climbed up on the couch and flopped next to me, panting slightly from the exertion. "Fuck, I thought you were having a seizure!" he said. "Did you know your eyes roll up in your head when you cum?"

"So I've been told," I said. This wasn't the first time I've heard that description of me having a *really* good orgasm! But I noticed it didn't stop him from finishing what he was doing. Fucking a girl having a seizure – that's not nice! Still, since I had enjoyed my *seizure* so much, I really had no choice but to forgive him and move on.

Tim's deposit seemed to leave me with a sense of calm. And fatigue. I leaned over and laid my head on his tummy, holding onto the damp, sticky, limp schlong with one hand, for emotional support. My eyes closed and I let the warm glow that comes from a successful conclusion – that much-desired *happy ending* – envelop me.

I'm not quite sure what happened after that. Those last 42 or 56 orgasms – I'm terrible at keeping track of the count – were kinda like a knockout punch. I guess I fell asleep, right there on the couch with Tim. I know we never made it up onto the bed to join in the orgy, which apparently petered out after Nikki sucked Mike off a second time. That's the problem when your orgy only has two guys and there are three horny gals with potentially as many as nine holes to be filled – the math doesn't work!

I vaguely remember saying goodbye to everyone at our front door. Tim kissed me, rubbed my pussy and told me how much he and the schlong had enjoyed meeting me. Next to us, Mike was engaged in pretty much the same activities with Bobbi and Nikki. Arthur, only recently awakened by Bobbi and still a bit on the groggy side, stood at the door, checking his watch and scratching his balls, no doubt wondering how all of us had become so chummy while he napped.

And then it was off to claim my final reward of the evening – sleep. I schlepped my drained, exhausted body down the hall and into our bed without brushing my teeth or washing up – I was too tired for that. By the time Mike showed up to join me, I was already asleep.

On Tuesday morning, I went over to Nikki's for coffee. Of course, eventually we ended up talking about what had happened Sunday at the barbecue. I believe I got that particular conversation started when I said, "So, did you have a good time fucking my boyfriend the other night?"

Nikki grinned and took a sip of her coffee. "Oh, yeah, I did. A *really* good time! I love sucking on that nice big dick of his."

"Yeah, so I've heard. Mike said you sucked him off twice."

"Well, it was just me and Bobbi. One of us had to do it. You're not jealous, are you? I saw you and Tim getting along pretty well."

"Nope. Not jealous. And you're right about Tim – he's a hunk."

"You know I've kinda got a thing for Mike. Right?"

"Yeah, I know."

"And you're still not jealous? How come?"

"Mike and I don't get jealous. We have that kind of relationship. Besides, he's not as much interested in you as you are in him – he just likes the way you suck cock."

"All the guys like the way I suck cock," she said. "I like it and I'm really good at it."

"That's true. But I know you, Nikki. Or rather, I've known girls like you. It's about conquest. Once you fuck Mike three or four more times, you'll lose interest and start looking for another guy to conquer."

"You think?"

"Yeah. So I'm not jealous. You'll move on and I'll still be with Mike."

"That's probably why I've had, like, 400 boyfriends in my life," Nikki said, laughing. "Always moving on."

"Could be," I said. I drank my coffee and took a bite of one of the cookies I'd brought along.

"So, ... why don't you let me do that today? Fuck him three or four more times, I mean. Then I can move on like you said and you can relax and not worry."

"I told you, I'm not worried. And as for that other thing, you'll have to work that out with him. You can screw him all you want, if he's up for it." I popped the rest of the cookie into my mouth, drained my coffee and said, "I gotta go. I've got things to do."

"Why don't you come over again tomorrow morning?" Nikki said. "I'll be planning out the Wednesday night show. Lots of new toys to show my *fans*."

"I dunno. Maybe." I headed for the door.

"Tim will be here."

I stopped and turned around. "You don't say?"

"Yeah. And maybe I could just run over and see what Mike is up to and leave you two alone for a while, if you know what I mean." She fluttered her eyelashes at me.

I couldn't help but laugh. "Really, Nikki, you're incorrigible!"

"Ooh, college girl knows big words."

"But a Wednesday morning partner swap?"

"It was only an idea," she said. "We don't have to do anything. Just c'mon over. We'll have fun."

"Okay, then. Well, I guess I'll see you in the morning," I said, and left.

"Bring more cookies," she called after me.

As I walked back across the street to my own house, I found myself thinking about Tim. I'd be glad to see him again – I found him sweet and sexy and I kinda liked him. And, knowing Nikki, I'd be willing to bet she had some devious plan to get us together so she could spend *quality time* with Mike. I wasn't sure how I felt about that, but I wasn't going to worry about it. *Que sera, sera,* and all that. I opened the door and let myself into the house, confident I could handle any and all surprises Wednesday morning might have in store for me.

the end – fini – owari

Hey! Get your hand out of your crotch! This story's over. But there are lots more of my stories about horny young men and juicy young women available at your favorite online bookstore. Check them out, and while you're at it,

please leave a (hopefully favorable) review. In the meantime, here's a sample from Book 5 of the <u>Mike and Melanie</u> series, as well as samples from Book 1 of my ongoing <u>Waikiki Hummer</u> series and Book 1 of my ongoing <u>Pleasantly Plump</u> series. Hope you like them.

The Pear Square Proposition
A Mike and Melanie Escapade – Book 5 (Sample)

I've got a problem. Have you ever heard that old joke, the one where a super-rich guy asks a girl, "Would you fuck me for a million bucks?" And the girl says, "Sure." Then the guys says, "How about for two bucks?" The girl says, "What do you think I am?" And the guy says, "I know what you are – you're a whore. Now we just need to agree on the price."

I find myself in a similar situation. A rich guy has offered me a lot of money to fuck him. A *lot* of money – $5,000 for one night of fucking and sucking. The thing of it is, I kinda like this guy and I'm strongly tempted to take him up on his offer. However, that would make me a whore, right? And I'm just not sure how I feel about that.

Let me tell you how all this came about.

A couple of months ago, a new and very cool coffee shop, *Java, Java, Java,* opened up about three blocks from here, on Kemperly Avenue. My neighbor, Nikki, and I went down there one morning to check it out and we really liked it. The coffee was delicious and reasonably priced and the vibe was casual and friendly. It almost felt as if you were visiting a friend's house.

The most enticing thing about the place, though, was their wide variety of super-scrumptious pastries, headlined by small, heavenly, tart-like squares of yummy, cinnamon-and-sugar goodness topped with pear halves, called *pear squares*. I'd never had them before and neither had Nikki, but once we tasted them, we were hooked. Pear squares had to be the most-delicious pastry in the entire universe!

Unfortunately for me and Nikki – and others, too, I assume – because of their popularity, the shop had put a limit of two on pear square orders. And take-out orders were not accepted – you could only get your two pear squares if you ordered them with coffee to consume on the premises. You'd better get there before the lunch crowd showed up, too, or there wouldn't be any left. So three or four mornings a week, Nikki and I would trek down the hill and head up Kemperly to our favorite coffee shop for our pear-square fix. And that's how I met Dennis Temley.

I'd seen him in here before. Several times, actually. He was tall and slender, perhaps 60 or 65 years old, with thinning gray hair and somewhat of a regal bearing. He frequently sat on a stool up by the counter, chatting up the owner, a young woman named Pam. He also spent a quite a bit of time checking out Nikki and me, trying to be sneaky about it but actually being somewhat obvious.

Anyway, on this particular morning – a Tuesday – Nikki and I were seated in our favorite spot, an old, overstuffed sofa on one side of the room, near the middle. We always sat there when the sofa was available. From there we could take in the whole room, survey the other customers, drink our coffee, eat our pear squares, and ... relax. Oh, and make up stories about the other coffee drinkers who populated the room.

"What about him?" Nikki said.

I looked up at the counter, where three or four people were milling about, waiting for their orders. "Which one?"

"The nervous-looking, shiny guy with the pointy shoes. Look at him – he's shiny all over. Shiny suit, shiny hair, the guy is just shiny everywhere."

"Probably a Mafia hit man, just in from Detroit on business," I said, taking a bite of my pear square.

"Obviously. He has 'Detroit' written all over him." Nikki agreed, scanning the rest of the room. "I see Mr. Rogers is here again."

"Who?"

"That old guy who sits up at the counter and is always checking us out."

"Is that his name? Mr. Rogers?"

"No, dummy," she said. "He reminds me of that children's show guy. I don't know what his real name is. He does look familiar, though."

"Of course he does. We see him in here all the time." I looked over at the counter, on the side near the wall, where 'Mr. Rogers' always sat. He was staring right at me and, as our eyes briefly made contact, he smiled. I quickly looked away and giggled.

"What?" Nikki said.

"He caught me looking at him. And he smiled at me."

"Ooh, a secret admirer. Did you smile back at him?"

"No. Why?"

"Because he's coming over here."

"What!" I cast a surreptitious glance in the direction of the counter and, sure enough, Mr. Rogers was heading right for us.

He walked up to the sofa and stood there, looking down at us, smiling. I peered up at him, expectantly, examining his face. His teeth were straight and white, much too nice for someone as ancient as he was. Crowns, probably. He also had a gorgeous tan. Up close, he projected the smell of money. Lots of money.

"Good morning, ladies," he said, bowing slightly. "I'm Dennis."

"Hi, Dennis," Nikki said. "I'm Nikki, and she's Mel – Melanie."

"Hello," I said to him. "And what can we do for you this fine morning, Dennis?"

"Well, I was hoping to speak with you," he said.

"And now you are," Nikki informed him.

He smiled at her. It really was a very attractive smile. "Yes. Yes, I am. Oh, and these are for you." He placed a white pastry bag on the coffee table in front of the sofa.

Nikki and I peeked in the bag. Pear squares! A bag full of pear squares!

"Don't tell anyone. These are to take home."

"Our lips are sealed, Dennis," Nikki said.

"Absolutely," I agreed. "No one will ever know. But how did you –"

"Get them? I have connections," he said, anticipating the rest of my question.

"Obviously," Nikki said.

"Pam's my granddaughter." He nodded toward Pam, busy making coffee, up behind the counter. "We're actually partners in this little adventure. But she's in charge. I'm more of a silent investor."

Well, that explained a lot. I'd always thought he was just a horny old guy, hitting on Pam, a girl young enough to be his, ... that's right, granddaughter! My opinion of him immediately improved upon hearing they were related.

"Why do you look so familiar to me?" Nikki said. "Are you famous or something?"

"I don't think so."

"What do you do?"

"I'm a – *was* a businessman. But I'm retired now."

"What's your last name, anyway?" Nikki said, continuing what sounded like an interrogation. Dennis, however, didn't seem to mind.

"It's Temley. I'm Dennis Temley."

Nikki looked thoughtful for a moment, then her face brightened. "Temley Industries? *That* Dennis Temley?"

"Yes, I'm afraid so."

"Shit! Don't be afraid," she said. "*That* Dennis Temley is the richest guy in this part of the state. And that's you, right?"

"Again, I'm afraid so." He projected a polite, almost formal air, but with decidedly friendly overtones.

"There it is again, that word. Afraid. Don't be afraid of it, Dennis. You're rich. Own it!"

He smiled. "So, I was wondering if I might pull up a chair and join you two for a bit?"

Nikki looked at me and I looked at her and then we both looked at Dennis. Had we discovered a pear-square connection? Hopefully.

"Sure. Take a load off," Nikki said.

"Have a seat," I said.

Dennis pulled a chair over and sat down, facing us, on the other side of the coffee table. "I see you in here quite frequently," he said.

"Yeah, we see you, too," Nikki said. "Always, like, checking us out." That's our Nikki – direct and to the point.

"I'm sorry. I don't mean to stare. But it's your friend, here." He indicated me. "Melanie, it it?"

"Mel," I told him.

"What's wrong with her?" Nikki wanted to know.

"Oh, nothing. Nothing at all. Here, let me show you something." He reached into his back pocket and took out a well-worn leather wallet, then extracted an old, faded, black and white photo and laid it on the coffee table. "Take a gander," he said. There's a word you don't hear much these days – gander.

Nikki picked up the photo and looked at it. "Holy shit! How old is this photo, anyways?"

"I think it was taken in 1963," he said.

"Holy shit!" she said again, and thrust the photo at me. "Take a look. It's you!"

Sure enough, the photo was a picture of me, looking pretty much the way I look right now. The only problem was, I was born in 1997. "What's going on?" I asked Dennis. "Who is this?"

"This is a picture of my late wife, Margie. Marjory. She was about 23 or 24 when this was taken, just before we got married."

"Wow, she looks just like you, Mel!" The look on Nikki's face was priceless. It was as if she'd just found out I was a time-traveler and was *very* surprised to hear the news.

I had to agree. The woman in the picture could have been my twin sister. That is, if you only considered looks and not the fact that my mother would have had to have been in labor for almost 60 years!

"So that's why you kept looking at us, huh?" Nikki said.

"Yes. That and, well, I was trying to get up enough nerve to come over here and talk to the two of you."

"Really?" I said. "We're not *that* scary, are we?"

"Oh, no. Not at all. But men are always somewhat intimidated by having to approach beautiful women, you know." He was looking straight at me when he said 'beautiful women' – not that surprising, I guess, considering he thought I looked just like his wife. Most husbands think their wives are beautiful, I think.

"Ooh, he thinks we're beautiful, Mel," Nikki said, and giggled.

"Don't mind her," I told Dennis. "She's a little bit goofy."

"It's all right. But you both are extremely attractive young women. There's no denying that."

"Thank you for the compliment, Dennis," I said, quickly, before Nikki could make a wisecrack.

"So, this is a little bit awkward, but I was wondering if I might have a word or two in private with you, Melanie?"

"What? You want me to leave?" Nikki said, pretending her feelings were hurt.

"Actually, I was hoping Melanie and I could go out to my car, where we could talk in private."

"Watch out, Mel. Sounds like a kidnapping plot to me. He's gonna get you in his car and then drive away with you. You remember what your mother told you when you were a little girl? Don't get into cars with strange men!"

"I'm not really that strange," Dennis said, still with a smile on his face. "And I don't drive, so I'm unlikely to drive away with your friend. Or roommate, or whatever."

"We're neighbors," I explained.

"You could be lying to us," Nikki observed.

Dennis turned and snapped his fingers. A large young man who was sitting at the counter hopped off his stool and in two seconds was standing next to us. He was really, *really* big – maybe like six-seven or six-eight and close to 300 pounds.

"This is Samuli – Sam," he said. "Sam, this is Melanie and Nikki. Say hi."

"Hello, ladies," Sam said.

I said "Hi," back and Nikki said, "Well, hel-lo, Sam. And my, aren't we a big boy!"

Before the always-horny Nikki could continue and invite Sam to have his way with her, right there on the sofa, Dennis interrupted. "Sam works for me. Tell them what you do, Sam."

"Whatever you tell me to do, sir. Mainly, though, I'm a driver – a chauffeur."

"So how about this, Nikki. I'll have Sam stay here with you while Melanie and I go have our private chat, and that way – without my driver – I won't be able to kidnap her."

"I was only kidding about that kidnapping thing, you know," she said. "But I'd be more than happy to stay here and, ... *entertain* Sam, so you two can talk in private."

"Thank you. So, Melanie, you seem to have your friend's permission. What about you? I promise I only want to talk to you. No kidnapping, no funny business, nothing. Just talk."

My curiosity was aroused. What did he want to talk to me about? "Sure, Dennis. Let's go talk."

"Wonderful."

"Take good care of my girl," I told Sam as we got up to leave. "Nikki, if I'm not back in 20 minutes, call the police."

Dennis laughed. "Yes. And tell them I've been kidnapped by a beautiful woman!"

"And remember, Nikki," I said, nodding toward Sam. "This is a public place. Don't get carried away."

She stuck her tongue out at me as Dennis and I walked away. Or maybe she was just showing it to Sam. With Nikki, it was impossible to tell.

Dennis's *car* turned out to be a black Mercedes limousine, parked in a private spot behind the shop. He held the door for me and we climbed into the back seat.

"This is some car," I observed, tumbling into an extremely soft bucket seat, one of four arranged around a small table. On the table were a laptop, a notebook and pens, and three phones. There was a TV overhead, or perhaps it was a monitor, and what appeared to be a small refrigerator was tucked between two of the seats.

"Yes. It's nice," he said, taking a seat across from me. "Would you care for some more coffee? Or pear squares? I can have Pam send some out, if you'd like."

"I'm good," I said. "So, ...?"

"Yes." He pushed a button on the table and a drawer slid out. From it, he extracted a white envelope, which he laid on the table. "There are 20 one-hundred-dollar bills in this envelope. They're for you," he said.

I had the feeling I'd just sat down into a James Bond movie and I was about to get an assignment. "Two thousand dollars? So, ... who do you want me to kill?"

And that's the end of this free sample of <u>The Pear Square Proposition: A Mike and Melanie Escapade, Book 5</u>. I wonder what's going to happen.

Will Melanie end up a hit-woman? And who does Dennis want her to kill, anyway? Or does he have something entirely different in mind? If you're curious, you can find out the answers to these pressing questions by downloading the book.

This next sample is from the first book of my ongoing <u>Waikiki Hummer</u> series, which I like to think of as an erotic-mystery-revenge thriller-adventure, sort of. This is definitely NOT a romance!

The Waikiki Hummer

A Waikiki Hummer Adventure – Book 1 (Sample)

Foreword

Terry Jean Rollins – TJ to her friends and The Waikiki Hummer to the rest of the world – is a cute, blonde, 23-year-old resident of Honolulu with only one ambition in life, to suck the cocks of as many shy, middle-aged, dorky male visitors to Waikiki as she can. She is a self-confessed dork lover who considers herself to be "maybe the best cocksucker in the entire world!" and dick-draining dorky tourists is her hobby. These are her stories, every one of them 110% true, according to her.

One

He was sitting in the center section of the bus, alone, leaning against the window, looking sad and forlorn, wearing horned-rim glasses and a really dorky-looking crew cut. *And,* there was a wedding ring on his finger. Perfect. Just what I was looking for.

Probably on his way to Ala Moana Center, I judged as I walked down the aisle toward him. When I got there, I said, "Mind if I sit next to you?" and flashed my friendliest smile.

He scooted over to give me more room, probably thinking it was odd I chose to sit next to him, since the bus was practically empty. But he said, "Fine," and smiled back at me.

I slid in beside him. "Here on vacation?" I said.

"Business. You?"

"I live here," I said.

"Lucky you." The way he said it made it sound as though his visit to Honolulu had so far been less than pleasurable. Given the chance, I hoped to change all that for him.

"Where you from?"

"Colorado. Denver."

"It sounds like you're not enjoying yourself here in our beautiful city."

"It's all right."

"How about your wife?" I pointed at his wedding ring. "I'll bet she likes it."

"She's not here. It's just me. Here on business."

Excellent! "How long is it, anyway?" I said.

He gave me a funny look. "What?"

"How long? Your business trip?"

"Oh. Two weeks. One more to go." He repeated the look. I couldn't quite tell what it meant. Apprehension, perhaps? Or maybe lust. I am, after all, not *that* bad looking. I wouldn't describe myself as beautiful – cute would probably be a better description. I've heard guys call me that. "She's a really cute girl," they'd say. And I think I agree with them. I *am* cute. I've got perky tits and a shapely ass and a really *friendly*-looking smile.

"I'm TJ," I said, and offered my hand.

"George," he said, shaking it with a slightly-damp palm.

When he released my hand, I let it drop down and land on his left thigh, just a few inches from his lap. He flinched slightly but left it there. I gave his thigh a tiny, almost-imperceptible squeeze.

"What do you like to do for excitement. George? What turns you on?" I flashed him that friendly smile once again.

"I play chess."

Excitement? Chess? That wasn't the kind of answer I'd been expecting.

"And golf. I'm a really good golfer."

Ooh, more excitement. "Really?"

"Yup. I've even won a couple of tournaments."

"You don't say." I gave his thigh another squeeze – a little harder this time – and slid my hand a couple of inches closer to his crotch. He looked down at it but didn't complain.

"What about you, TJ?"

"Me?"

"Yeah. What do you do for excitement? What are your hobbies?"

This conversation wasn't heading in the direction I'd intended. My new friend, George, seemed to be a little slow on the uptake. I decided I needed to be more direct. "I only have one hobby," I told him.

"And? What is it?"

I turned and leaned closer to him and put my mouth up close to his ear. Then, in my best sexy-sounding voice, I whispered, "I like to suck cock." As I said it, I switched hands on his thigh and slid my left hand the rest of the way up his thigh, into his crotch, and grabbed his cock through his pants. Surprise, surprise – it was already rock-hard. Maybe George wasn't as slow as he seemed.

His eyebrows shot up about 14 inches. "What?" he said, turning to look at me.

"I like to pick up strange men – almost always tourists – and go to their hotel with them and then give them the best blowjob they've ever had in their entire life. It's my specialty. Blowjobs." I smiled and squeezed his cock several more times.

"How much?" George said.

"What?" I didn't understand the question.

"How much do you charge?"

I pulled my head back and gave him my best *disappointed* look. "Really, George? You think I'm a hooker? Look at me. Look at how I'm dressed." My outfit of the day consisted of white shorts, a baby-blue T-shirt and rubber *zoris* instead of shoes.

"Have you seen the hookers in this town, George? They're cruising Waikiki every night, strolling up and down Kalakaua, asking tourists if they'd like a *date*. Their skirts are four inches long and the heels of their shoes are twice that."

"I've seen 'em." he said.

I squeezed his cock again – hard, this time – and didn't release it for several seconds. "It's a hobby with me, George. I just like sucking dick. It makes me feel ... oh, I don't know. Powerful, I guess." *Yeah. Taking that stiff dick and turning it into a soft little lump of flesh with the consistency of a limp dishcloth, it makes me feel powerful.*

"I see."

"And I especially like strange men."

"Strange? You think I'm strange?"

"Not strange weird. Strange like we don't know each other."

"Oh."

"So, ...?"

"No charge?"

"Nope."

"All right. I'm up for it," he said.

"Obviously," I said, pointing at his pants, which now featured a tent where the fly was. "You'd better carry something in front of that when we get off the bus."

"I'll do that." He smiled, picked his briefcase up off the floor and held it up for me to see.

"Perfect," I told him.

Two

The hotel where George was staying was not one of the fancy, beachfront, super-expensive tourist traps fronting Kalakaua Avenue with back doors that open up right onto the beach. I guess I should have expected that, since George had said he was here on business, not as a tourist. Anyway, it was on a side street, almost three blocks up from the beach, near Ala Wai Boulevard and the canal.

We had to hail a cab after we got off the bus. George's hotel was back down at the other end of Waikiki, the Diamond Head end. The driver who stopped to pick us up wasn't too happy about the fact we were only going a few blocks but George promised him a big tip and when we got there, he gave him a twenty and told him to keep the change. The cabbie thanked us and drove off with an extra-large smile on his face.

George's room was on the ninth floor, with a view of Ala Wai Boulevard, Ala Wai Canal, and the Ala Wai Golf Course on the other side of the canal. With the exception of the lanai – which I doubted got much use because of the constant winds swirling around this area – it was just a standard hotel room like you might find in any business hotel in any large city. There was a double bed, a desk and chair, a dresser, an armchair, a medium-size flat-screen TV and, of course, a bathroom and a place to hang clothes. Nothing fancy, but then, we weren't here for the décor, anyway.

"What now?" George said, turning to face me.

"Why don't you take off some of those clothes? Honolulu's too hot to be wearing a suit."

"Yeah, you're right. It *is* hot." He started removing his clothes, tossing them onto the armchair while at the same time casting nervous glances in my direction.

"Relax, George," I told him, adding a slight chuckle. "I'm not going to hurt you. I'm not going to rob you or yell rape or anything like that. I just want to suck your cock. It's my hobby, it's what I do for fun."

"Strange hobby," he said.

He had stripped down to just his boxer shorts and socks by this time and was trying to remove his socks by hopping on one foot while he pulled a sock off the other foot. It wasn't going that well – he was hopping all over the room, trying to maintain his balance. When he hopped by me, I reached out and pushed him over backwards, onto the bed, and pulled off both socks for him.

"Thanks," he said, looking up at me from his recumbent position.

"Wouldn't want you to hurt yourself before we get to the fun part." I hopped up on the bed and slid up close to him, with my head on his right shoulder and my right arm draped over his chest. "Comfy?" I said.

"Uh-huh."

"Good." I stretched my head up and began to nibble on his right ear. At the same time my right hand slithered down his body until it landed on top of his once-again-rock-hard cock, but outside his boxer shorts. I let it rest there, separated from his dick by just a thin layer of cotton, without doing anything – no squeezing, no stroking, nothing – while I continued to chew on his ear.

He shivered.

"Relax, George. You're gonna like this. I promise."

"I think I already like it."

"It gets better," I said. I slipped my hand under the waistband of his shorts and wrapped my fingers around his dick, giving it a couple of light squeezes – what I like to think of as *introductory* squeezes or *How do you do?* squeezes.

George moaned and said, "Fuck, that feels good!"

"Take off your shorts," I told him.

He reached down and, with just a little help from me, slipped his boxers down over his hips and onto his legs, from where he kicked them off. His cock – six inches of thick, beautiful man-meat – stared up at me, wavering up and down, practically wearing a *Please hurry up and do me* sign. I smiled, thinking *that's what I'm here for,* leaned down and sucked that beautiful purple-headed shaft into my mouth.

George seemed to like that. I swirled my tongue slowly around the head of his dick, occasionally licking upward on the bottom of the shaft, only to concentrate again on the head. Any girl who's sucked a few cocks will tell you that's where the action is – the dickhead. The shaft is really only there so you'll have something to hang onto while you're working on the head.

Apparently, though, it had been a long while since George had been laid or gotten his dick gobbled, because I was just getting started, just warming up, when I felt his cock go super-hard and begin to spasm. I put my tongue on the bottom of his dickhead, wiggled it back and forth slowly, and began to gently suck.

A warm stream of cum – my tasty reward, as I usually liked to think of it – spurted out onto my tongue, followed by a slight pause and then two more spasmodic ejections. I sucked it all up and swallowed, never letting go of his dick. But it wasn't just George's dick doing the spasm thing. His whole body shook and he arched his back each time he pumped a load into my mouth. He commented out loud on it, too. He went, "Oh! Oh! Oh!' and "Oh!"

I spit his dick out into my hand and hung onto it, massaging it gently as I watched him gasping for air, trying to catch his breath. He really wasn't in the best of shape for a guy – what, forty or fifty years old? The thought crossed my mind I might have some explaining to do if old George had a heart attack and croaked on me.

"Shit! I'm so sorry," he said when he was able to breathe normally again.

"Don't worry about it," I said, laughing. "We're not finished yet."

"No?"

"No." Actually, this – getting a load of warm jizz shot into my mouth 30 seconds or so after I start sucking a strange guy's cock – happened to me a lot. But I was never disappointed. I liked to think it was because I was such a skillful cocksucker I could get any guy to cum in record time. And also, I knew we were just getting started. If George thought that shooting one little load of cum down my throat was the end of this adventure, he was in for a big, big surprise.

I've always thought of cocksucking as an art form, something to be done slowly and gracefully, leisurely, sensually stroking and licking your way toward a tasty treat until a stream of warm, delicious cum – the reward – fills your mouth and rolls down your throat. When done right, it can take hours, with the reward being repeated two and sometimes three times, until that poor, pitiful penis is completely wasted, of no good to any woman for several days. And that's what I intended to do to George – suck his cock so dry it would be useless for the next week or so!

Three

I let George rest while I entertained myself playing with his dick and giving it an occasional wet, slurpy lick, just to keep him interested. When I was younger, I used to wish I was a boy so I'd have a dick to play with whenever I wanted, but as I got older I realized that wasn't necessary. Any reasonably decent-looking girl could pretty much find a cock to play with any time she wanted. Usually, all you had to do was ask.

After 15 or 20 minutes of me diddling with it, George's dick had re-inflated to a sort of floppy, spongy fullness – not really hard but on its way. During the entire time, he only said two things to me, "I like that," and "Are you for sale? I want to buy you and take you home with me." The rest of the time he just moaned.

I thought I knew a way to speed things up. I used my hand to milk his cock for a minute or two, then leaned over, put it in my mouth and began massaging the tip – just the top part of his dickhead – with my tongue. At the same time I began to hum.

"What the hell?" George propped himself up on both elbows and gazed at me, looking slightly alarmed. "What are you doing?"

I pulled his cock out of my mouth, making an exaggerated smacking sound as I did so. "Round two," I told him.

"No, I mean that noise. That buzzing sound. What was that?"

Keeping George's cock in my hand, I sat back on my haunches. "I was humming."

A puzzled look slid across his face, replacing the alarm. "Why?"

I shrugged. "I like it. It's my thing. I like to hum while I suck cock."

"You're kidding!"

"Nope." To prove it to him, I leaned forward, popped his dick back into my mouth, and hit him with about 20 seconds of the Australian folk song, *Waltzing Matilda.* When I spit his dick back out into my hand, it was quite a bit firmer than when it had gone in. Also larger. "See? Guys like it, too," I said.

"Is it always that song?" he asked me.

"Nope. I mix 'em up. Why? You got a favorite song you want me to hum for you?"

"Yeah. *In the Still of the Night.*"

"Shit, how old *are* you, anyway? Damn, George, that song's like a hundred years old."

"I know, but I can't help it. I like fifties music. And that's one of my favorites. Do you know it?"

"The Five Satins, right?"

"Yeah."

"I think I do." I leaned back down and slurped his dick – still only at about half-mast but trying hard to make it up to the crow's nest – into my mouth, lightly sucking and tonguing the tip as I began to hum *In the Still of the Night.*

And then a funny thing happened. As I was working my tongue in a circular motion around the head of George's cock, humming his favorite song and forcing that cock into a more-rigid state, he began to sing along with me. Pretty loudly, in fact.

Trouble was, George wasn't much of a singer. In fact, he was fucking terrible! But I knew just the cure for that. I rolled over to one side and removed my shorts and panties, then climbed back on top of him. Temporarily abandoning his almost totally firmed-up dick for the moment, I crawled up his body until my crotch was about an inch from his face.

"You like pussy, George?" I asked him.

"I do."

"Take a good look, then. Freshly washed, carefully shaved, just a nice, clean, smooth, moist pussy, with no hair to get in your mouth and spoil that creamy goodness." I moved a little forward, grabbed him by the ears and gently pulled his head upward. Just a bit. Then I lowered my cunt – now juicy with anticipation – onto his waiting mouth, grinding it against his lips before releasing his ears and spreading open my pussy with my fingers to make sure his tongue would have easy access to my clit.

Oh, too bad. That's the end of this sample of The Waikiki Hummer, Book 1. *And just when things were starting to get interesting, too. But TJ's time with George is almost up and she's about to get involved with Tony, a bad guy from the mainland who's definitely* not *her type. And when she* accidentally *ends up in possession of a large amount of counterfeit twenty-dollar bills, both trouble and fun ensue as she tries to give them back without getting herself killed! I don't want to give the rest of the story away – it's a good one. Download the book to find out what happens.*

Meanwhile, here's a sample from another one of my ongoing series. These stories are best described as erotic – highly *erotic – romances. This sample is the opening of book one.*

Jennifer's Story
Pleasantly Plump (Sample)

"I am *not* fat!" I told my full-length bathroom mirror as I climbed out of the shower. I'd caught it staring at me.

This is the part where, in the movies, the mirror answers back and says something like, "Well, *I* certainly didn't say anything." But my mirror evidently had no acting skills. It just sat there, staring at me, never saying a word.

"I'm soft and curvy, with beautiful, full titties, a nice, round ass, and a pussy that deserves way better than I get from David," I continued, repeating the affirmation I'd written for myself and was now required to repeat at least 10 times a day, according to the online *Pussy Power* course I was taking.

Every word of that affirmation was true. A lot of guys would put me in the category known as *Pretty Fucking Hot*, I was sure. But not David. With him it was always, *Hey, babe, why don't you try to lose a few pounds?* or, *You putting on weight, sweetie?* frequently followed by a slap on the ass.

And all because of an extra five or ten pounds of baby fat. Hell, I'm only 20 years old. In a couple of years that will be gone, as if by magic, and I'll be just about perfect. Which is what David wants, apparently.

I've never really understood that. Why some guys are so into screwing those skinny, bony model-types, I mean. That couldn't be a lot of fun for either of them, clanging their hip bones together as they pumped away. You'd think those guys would rather be lying on a soft, warm body with a little padding. Like mine.

Anyway, if *wham-bam-thank-you-ma'am* David was doing the screwing, there wasn't much to worry about, I guess. He was seldom in the saddle long enough to do any real damage. That thought brought a smile to my lips as I got dressed, followed by a frown as I realized that's all I ever really got from him – a quickie. David was almost always a quick, unsatisfying fuck, at least for me.

Too bad he couldn't be more like Alejandro. Alejandro knew how to treat a woman, both in and out of bed. He was kind and gentle, as well as being tall, dark and mysterious, muscular, and handsome. And, best of all, perhaps, he was equipped with eight inches of the smoothest, most beautiful, most delicious man-meat possible – a cock that would more than satisfy just about any girl.

Only trouble was, Alejandro wasn't real. He was a sweet vision, existing only in my head, a guy I'd invented years ago. He was the guy I imagined each time I gave my vibrator a workout.

Yeah, my vibrator, my wonderful vibrator. A vibrating dildo, actually. The only time my pussy ever got any real action was when I broke out that old, eight-inch fake cock I bought myself for my nineteenth birthday. I ordered it online and didn't realize how long it was. And *thick*, too. That little jewel took some getting used to – a thick eight inches was a tight fit. But it fits better now, thanks to lots of practice over the past year or so. Which reminded me – I needed to replace it. The silicone was beginning to peel off from overuse.

I'd definitely gotten my money's worth from it, though. Maybe I'll order the six-speed, 10-inch monster dong, this time, I thought. That's the one with the little clit-rubbing extension on one side and a mini-dick sticking out the other side, so you can fuck yourself in the pussy and the ass at the same time, if you want to. I'm not sure I'll be using it that way on a regular basis, but I'll definitely give it a try because I once had a guy stick his finger up my ass while he was pounding my pussy and I came almost immediately. That was one of the best orgasms I ever had!

My phone rang and I picked it up. "Hey, what's up?" I said to my best friend, Marlene. We've been friends since elementary school and she calls me two or three mornings a week at about this time, to "check in," as she phrases it, but I sometimes think she calls me just to see if I'm still alive.

"Wha'cha doin'?" she said.

"Nothing. Getting dressed. Talking to my mirror."

"Yeah? About what?"

"You know – David, guys, the fact that I haven't had a good screwing in over a month. That kind of shit."

Marlene laughed. "I can't believe a dick-friendly girl like you can't find a guy to give her a good fuck."

"What makes you think I'm *that* dick-friendly?"

"You like dicks, don't you?"

"Well, duh! Of course. Where would the world be without dicks?" I said, laughing.

"That makes you dick-friendly. If you like them, you have to be friendly to them."

It was tough to argue with that logic. "I guess," I said.

"So, listen, you wanna go to a flick tonight?"

"Can't. I've got a date with David."

"Oh." Marlene didn't much care for David. Although she'd never actually told me she didn't like him, I could tell from the way she reacted whenever I mentioned him that she thought I could do better.

"Maybe some other night?" I suggested. "This is more like a business meeting than a date. Some college friend of David's is moving here and David wants to help him buy a house, or rent an apartment, or something. So the three of us are going out for drinks." David was a real estate agent, so this was both a business meeting and a college reunion of sorts.

"Yeah, okay. Some other night, then. Anyway, I gotta go. Just wanted to check in."

"I'm still alive," I told her.

"That's good," she said, and hung up.

I finished dressing and headed off to school, where I was already five minutes late for my psych class.

David showed up at eight, right on time, as always. "Ready?" he said.

"Yup. Let's go." I turned off my lights and we headed down the steps to his car.

"You look nice tonight," he said, as he opened the car door and held it for me.

Whoa! What the fuck was that? A compliment from David – I must have misheard him. I've worn this outfit a dozen times before and he's never said a word about it. "Thanks," I said, climbing in. "You look nice, too."

He grinned and closed the door, then got in the other side and we left, heading for – well, I didn't know where we were going. David hadn't mentioned it.

"Where's this friend of yours? I thought he was going to have drinks with us."

"Yeah, he is. Al – that's his name, Al – said he'd meet us there."

Al? Could that be short for Alejandro? I smiled inwardly at the thought. "Where's *there*? Where are we going?" I said.

"Dottie's. I told him we'd meet him there at around eight-thirty."

Of course. Dottie's Den, David's favorite bar and grille. Tiny little tables with tiny little lamps putting out so little illumination you couldn't see the high prices on the menu. Watery drinks, crappy food and rude, snarky servers – what's not to like? Plus, there was an overall *damp* feeling to the place. I hated it.

We got there early – Dottie's was only 10 or 12 blocks from my place. The dining room was pretty much empty, about normal for a weekday night. We skipped through to the lounge, also just about empty, and grabbed a booth with a view of the entrance. I've always wondered how this place stays in business. Every time we've been here it's been like this – empty. Of course, we always come during the week because David is so busy on weekends, what with open houses and stuff. They probably did a shitload of business on weekends, was my guess.

"What's this friend of yours look like?" I said, after we'd ordered and our drinks had come.

"He's tall. Dark. He's from Mexico, I think. Or Colombia. Someplace in South America. Yeah, Colombia, maybe."

"Don't you know? I thought you were friends."

"Yeah, well, more like acquaintances, really. I know him from school and he knows I'm in real estate, so he contacted me."

Hmm. Tall, dark, and Hispanic. Just like Alejandro. I took a big gulp of the illegally-served, watery screwdriver in front of me and began to fantasize about the mysterious Al from Mexico. Or Colombia. Or someplace in South America.

"That's him," David said, interrupting my reverie.

I looked up and practically choked. The large, muscular man walking toward us with a huge smile on his dark face looked almost exactly like my fantasy man – the man who filled my thoughts while I rode my dildo – Alejandro.

Fuck! Was this possible? Maybe I was dreaming. Yeah, that had to be it. I fell asleep on my couch, waiting for David, and now I was dreaming. But I wasn't dreaming, so I stood up, along with David, to greet him.

David introduced us. "Al Entavez, this is my main squeeze, Jennifer," he said.

That really pissed me off. Him calling me his 'main squeeze,' I mean. I wasn't anybody's 'squeeze,' main or otherwise. Least of all David's. David was just a temporary distraction, someone who was supposed to make me happy for a while and then move on. And he wasn't doing a very good job of it.

"Well, *hel-lo*, Jennifer," Al said, taking my hand in his. He stepped back and took a good long look at me, eyeing me from head to toe as David looked on, beaming. A weak feeling slid into my knees.

"David told me he was bringing his girlfriend tonight," Al continued, "but he failed to mention she was a model. A *very* beautiful model." That weak feeling left my knees and slithered up my inner thighs.

"Always the kidder," David commented, sitting back down.

Fuck you, David.

Al was still standing there, holding my hand in his and eyeballing me in a decidedly non-kidding manner. I could feel the warmth creeping up my neck and knew I was blushing, so I did the only thing I could think of. I shook his hand, said, "Thank you for the compliment, Al," and sat back down.

"Call me Alex," he said, sitting down beside me. "I prefer that to Al."

Alex. All right. I'd been hoping that Al was short for Alejandro, but what the hell – Alex was a perfectly nice name. I was also a little disappointed that Alex had no noticeable accent. He sounded like an American. The Alex of my fantasies – whoops, I meant the *Alejandro* of my fantasies – always told me how hot I was in a really sexy Hispanic accent. Oh, well, as the song goes, *You Can't Always Get What You Want.*

David didn't waste any time rehashing their college years or catching up on more recent events in their lives – he got right to work. "So, you're looking for a place here in Orlando, huh? You wanna rent or buy?"

Alex turned his attention away from me and toward the task at hand – finding a place to live. "I guess I'd like to rent for about a year, get used to the community, you know, then buy a place."

"Excellent way to go about it," David said. "I can help you with that."

I sipped my drink and tuned them out, losing myself in fantasies about Alex. Or Alejandro. I wasn't sure which of them I was daydreaming about, since the two men were practically identical, but I was just getting to a good part when David's phone rang, snapping me back to reality.

"What, now?" I heard him say, followed by a period of silence. Then, "Shit, Joan, it's almost nine o'clock. I'm in a bar."

A longer silent period followed, presumably while Joan, the office manager at David's company, explained whatever had caused this interruption.

"All right, all right. Fifteen minutes," he said, and hung up.

"Something wrong?" Alex said.

"Crap! I'm sorry – I've gotta go to the office."

"Now?" both Alex and I said at the same time.

"Yeah. Look, I'll only be gone a half-hour. I've just gotta sign some papers that need to be delivered by eight o'clock tomorrow morning. Take me two minutes and then I'll come right back. You guys just stay here, have a couple of drinks, get to know one another or whatever, and I'll be back before you know it. Okay?"

Alex tossed a quick, smiling glance in my direction, then turned back to David and said, "Sure. No problem." I nodded my agreement, as if I really had a say in what David intended to do.

"Great, then." He drained his glass, offered us a final, "I'll be back in a jif," and left.

And that's the end of the sample of <u>Jennifer's Story.</u> Darn! Just when it was starting to get interesting, too. I'd be willing to bet that leaving Jennifer and Alex alone at Dottie's Den turns out to be a bad move for David, but ... who knows what might happen? Of course, you can always find out by downloading the book.

Well, that's it. I hope you enjoyed the book and the previews. If you haven't done so already, please don't forget to leave a review for this book, *Backyard Barbecue – A Mike and Melanie Escapade, Book 4.*

See ya soon, I hope! Shannon